BOYS CAMP

BOYS CAMP

Nate's Story

Written by Kitson Jazynka
Illustrated by Craig Orback

**Every boy has
a great story.**

Sky Pony Press
New York

Sky Pony Press books may be purchased in bulk at special discounts for sales promotion, corporate gifts, fund-raising, or educational purposes. Special editions can also be created to specifications. For details, contact the Special Sales Department, Sky Pony Press, 307 West 36th Street, 11th Floor, New York, NY 10018 or info@skyhorsepublishing.com.

Sky Pony® is a registered trademark of Skyhorse Publishing, Inc.®, a Delaware corporation.

Visit our website at www.skyponypress.com.

10 9 8 7 6 5 4 3 2 1

Manufactured in China, July 2013
This product conforms to CPSIA 2008

Catalog in publication data is available on file.
ISBN: 978-1-62087-981-8

Bird card illustrations courtesy of the Smithsonian Migratory Bird Center. Artwork by John C. Anderton.

Boys Camp is grateful to Andrew Knotts for his wonderful sketches of the owl and the cowbirds and for his handwritten notes. Thanks, Andrew! You really gave us a hand!

Have fun. Make friends. Be yourself.

Hello, Camper!

All of us at Camp Wolf Trail are looking forward to greeting you on July 10. We've got a great summer ahead of us.

Pretty soon you'll be packing your trunk for your two weeks here at camp. If this is your first summer at Wolf Trail, you're probably curious—and maybe even a little nervous—about what to expect, especially if this is your first time away from home.

Well, first of all, don't worry. Camp is fun. And here at Wolf Trail, we've been sharing the fun with kids like you for more than fifty years.

As soon as you arrive, counselors and returning campers will welcome you and help you find the way to your cabin. The cabins are are scattered like acorns throughout the woods. You'll be sharing your cabin with eight other campers and two counselors.

Counselors and campers of different ages are assigned to groups called "clusters." Together, you and your cluster will come up with a funny name and a signature move for your group. You'll take turns doing communal chores, like setting the table for eighty hungry monkeys (also known as the campers, counselors, and camp staff). You and your cluster will compete against other clusters during our camp theme days, including the Oddball Championships. Past themes have been Martian Day, Rock Star Day, Backwards Day, Half Magic Day, and Chicken-of-the-Woods Day.

Every day there are lots of activities to choose from: swimming in clear, cool Evergreen Lake, boating, canoeing, arts and crafts, hiking, sports, and trail blazing (also known as bushwhacking). At night everyone at camp gathers around a fire for songs, stories, jokes, and reflection. And each week you and your fellow campers and counselors will go off on a wilderness adventure into the woods, over the mountains, or even across the lake, with only what you'll need to survive for two nights and three days. You'll rest on breezy overlooks, discover secret, hidden swimming spots, cook over a campfire, and sleep out under the stars, listening to owls hooting. Your counselors have been doing this for years and will look forward to teaching you the ways of the wilderness.

You are in for a wonderful time! So, pack your enthusiasm and your sense of humor along with your socks, and come to Camp Wolf Trail. We are ready for the fun to begin, and we know that you are too.

See you soon!

All of us here at Camp Wolf Trail

Packing List

Due to our simple camp lifestyle, and our even-more-rustic wilderness trips, anything you bring may get wet, dirty, lost, or all three combined. So, leave the special stuff at home.

Do bring:
Daily camp supplies
☐ Shorts and T-shirts for warm weather

☐ Clothes for cooler temperatures (Fleece clothing is good for camping because it dries quickly.)

☐ Socks (Wool is good for hiking because it also dries quickly.)

☐ Hiking shoes or boots for trips, and everyday shoes for camp (Be sure to break in new boots or shoes before you get here!)

☐ Old sneakers/water shoes for canoeing and creek hikes

☐ Swimming gear: suit, sunscreen, towel

☐ Sheets, blanket, and pillow for your bunk in camp

☐ Bathroom items: towel, toothbrush, toothpaste, shampoo, soap (although we've noticed that some campers' soaps don't get used too often!)

Wilderness trip supplies
☐ The basics: a comfortable backpack, lightweight sleeping bag, roll-up camping pad, mess kit (plate, cup, fork, and spoon) water bottle, flashlight with extra batteries, waterproof poncho

☐ Optional: camping knife (check it in with your counselor

when you arrive), camping pillow, compass, hat, bandanna

☐ If you wear glasses, bring a cord to hold them safely around your neck, so you don't lose them when boating or rock climbing.

Other optional items

☐ Good books

☐ Portable games such as cards and cribbage, crossword puzzles

☐ Paper, stamps, envelopes, pen, addresses (Your parents and friends will want to hear from you!)

☐ Art supplies, journal, nature guides, binoculars, musical instrument (if it's not too fragile), or other hobby supplies

☐ Pocket money (no more than $20, though)

Please **do not bring** any electronics or a cell phone. They don't survive getting wet, dirty, or lost. And besides, who needs them? You'll be hiking in the woods and swimming in the lake most of the time. Who would you text? A squirrel? A fish? Enjoy being free of screens (except the kind that keeps bugs out) for two weeks!

BOYS CAMP

Nate's Story

Chapter One

"Say what?" asked Nate, jolted into focus.

"Earth to Nate," said Vik. "I said, do you want this?" He offered Nate a marshmallow so burnt that it looked like a lump of coal.

"Thanks, but I'll pass," said Nate, grinning. "Besides, I thought you were going for the World Record for Marshmallow Intake."

"Yeah," sighed Vik, "but I'm having an off night. This would only be my twelfth. But my teeth are starting to itch. You're sure you—"

Hoo, hoo. Nate twisted around, looking at the woods behind him. *So that's where you are,* he thought. *I'm coming to find you, Owl.* He stood and zipped up his hooded sweatshirt.

"Yo," said Vik. "Where are you going?"

"I'm, uh . . ." Nate hesitated. At school, kids teased him about how he liked birds. That's why Nate was still keeping his interest in birds a secret, even from Vik.

When Nate didn't finish his sentence, Vik said, "Relax, buddy. You can't go anywhere. You and I are on fire duty, remember?"

"Oh, yeah," said Nate. He sank back down, glancing over his shoulder at the woods.

"What's back there that's got you so jumpy?" asked Vik.

"Nothing," said Nate. Then he decided to trust Vik—a little. "It's just, I heard an owl, and I sort of want to see it."

"Okay, so after we douse the campfire, we can go look for it," said Vik. He tossed the stick and the marshmallow into the fire.

"Really?" asked Nate, surprised. "You want to?"

"Sure," said Vik. "We'll hunt for you-know-who-oo-oo."

Vik's hoot was pretty loud, but no one else heard him because the other campers were singing.

Nate laughed. "Okay," he said. "You're on."

"Hey, Nate," Vik said. "Knock, knock."

"Who's there?"

"I hope so," said Vik. "Get it?"

"Oh, man, that's painful," groaned Nate. He shoved two uncooked marshmallows in his ears.

Now Vik laughed. Vik was a newbie; it was his first summer at Camp Wolf Trail. Nate had hit it off with Vik right away, and he was really glad that they were both in Birch Cabin along with his friends from last summer: Yasu, Jim, Erik, and Zee, and the other newbies, Zack, Kareem, and Sean.

"All right, everybody," said Simon, one of the counselors. "That wraps up the show for tonight."

Another counselor, Carlos, lifted the strap of his guitar off of his shoulder and started to put it in its case. "Time to hit the sack, boys."

Nate leapt to his feet, tossing his ear marshmallows into the flames. He was eager to put out the fire and be on his way.

But most of the other campers didn't want to leave. "Noooooo," they groaned. "One more song! One more song!"

Carlos held up his hands in surrender. "Okay," he said. "You got it. One more song on the condition that you sing it as you follow me back to your cabins. Deal?"

"Deal!" yelled the campers.

Nate glanced at the woods. He hoped the noise wouldn't scare the owl away. It might be a screech owl, or maybe a great horned.

Carlos strummed his guitar. "You'll be sorry," he said to the campers with a mischievous look. "I'm gonna sing the goofiest song I know." He took a deep breath, and sang at the top of his voice:

You put your right foot in,
You put your right foot out . . .

The campers laughed and howled with glee and soon everyone was singing the "Hokey Pokey" as they danced—*left foot in, left foot out*—behind Carlos through the woods to the cabins. As the

last *That's what it's all about* faded away, Nate was glad that most of the cabins were in the opposite direction from where he thought the owl might be.

At the lake, Nate filled two buckets with water and Vik filled a bucket with sand. They lugged the buckets to the fire circle, and then Nate dumped the water on the fire, making the flames hiss and smoke and sputter out. Vik grabbed a stick and stirred the soupy gray slurry. He dumped the bucket of sand in the slop to finish the job.

"Thanks, guys," said Simon. He poked a large stick into the mess that used to be a blazing campfire to make sure the fire was really out. Fire was a serious danger at Camp Wolf Trail, since all the cabins were made of wood. "I'm headed to a meeting up at the dining hall," said Simon. "I'll see you two back at Birch."

"Got it," said Nate.

"See ya, Simon," said Vik. After Simon walked away, Vik clicked on his flashlight, held it under his chin so that it cast a weird light on his face, and asked Nate in a ghoulish voice, "Still up for finding the owwww-ellll?"

"You bet," said Nate. "No doubt about it."

"Tell me how you really feel," joked Vik. "By the way, are you sure we're allowed to do this? Take a nighttime stroll, I mean."

Nate pulled up his hood and shrugged. "Technically, we're just taking the scenic route back to our cabin, right?"

Vik nodded. "I guess."

Hoo, hoo.

"That owl's calling us," Nate said. "Let's go."

Nate led the way into the woods, swinging his lit flashlight low on the path to light the way for his feet. At eleven years old, Nate was big for his age, especially his feet, hands, and ears. Vik— the same age—was short and skinny, and usually sported a beat-up old tennis visor. The boys said nothing as they followed a pine-needly, winding path that led away from the fire circle. The cabins at Camp Wolf Trail were sprinkled throughout the woods so campers were truly living in the forest for two weeks. Off to the far left as they passed, Nate and Vik could see flashlights from inside Spruce Cabin and Paw Paw Cabin flickering through the pine trees like lightning bugs.

Cicadas chirped and mosquitoes hummed, but it was mostly quiet in the woods this late at night. In the morning, campers woke to a racket of birds and insects and hungry deer grazing in the trees outside their cabins. There were other wild animals too: raccoons, skunks, quick cottontail rabbits, and squirrels. Even a bobcat had wandered through camp once. Old campers claimed to have seen black bears, and Nate figured there must have been at least one wolf—sometime—whose trail had given the camp its name.

Walking along in the dark with Vik, Nate thought about how much he loved Camp Wolf Trail. Camp meant two weeks of endless hikes, no set bedtime, kayaking across Evergreen Lake, and being outdoors all day long. To Nate, who was always curious about stuff, camp meant a million new things to notice, and to wonder about, and to ask himself questions about. And camp meant friends and lots of *time* with friends. Camp was staying up late and talking about anything and everything with everybody. *Well, almost*, Nate corrected himself. *Not birds. Not yet. Not everybody.*

Behind him, Nate heard Vik stumble. "You okay, Vik?" he asked.

"Yeah," Vik answered. "I've got nine other toes, so no problem."

"Because you don't have to do this," Nate said.

"No, I'm good," said Vik.

Nate was glad. Hunting for the owl all by himself wouldn't have been as much fun.

The boys walked in silence for a while. Nate craned his neck, looking in the high branches for the owl.

"So, I didn't know you were into owls," said Vik. "You like raptors?"

Seems like the time has come to tell Vik the whole truth, Nate thought. So he said, "Well, I . . . yeah, I mean, I like *all* birds."

One of the things Nate liked best about Vik was how quick he was with jokes. So Nate braced himself now, in case Vik made a joke about birds. He was still mad about the way last year at school, back when his interest in birds began, kids had made fun of him and said he was dorky.

But good old Vik didn't say anything jokey or snarky, so Nate went on: "I'm keeping a list of birds I see. I sketch them too." He patted his back pocket. "In this notebook."

"Aw, man!" said Vik. "That's what that notebook's for? I noticed it, but I thought you were writing down all my great jokes."

"Nope," said Nate, relieved and happy at Vik's reaction. "Sorry. Just birds. The kids at school call me Bird Nerd."

"Typical," said Vik. "I'd say they're bird *brains*, but I don't want to stoop to their level."

Nate laughed. "Anyway, that's why I don't talk about the bird notebook. I'm tired of being razzed."

"Hey, we've all got secrets," said Vik.

"Oh, yeah?" Nate started to ask. "What's your—?"

But Vik talked over him, saying, "That's something I like a lot about Camp Wolf Trail: camp's not school. Nobody here knows your school stuff or team stuff or home stuff or whatever. You can leave all that behind."

"Right," said Nate. Whatever Vik's secret was, it was clear that he didn't want to talk about it.

"So, is keeping the list like a competition or something?" Vik asked. "The guy who sees the most birds wins?"

"Nah," said Nate. "I just do it to do it."

"Cool," said Vik.

Nate stopped next to a break in the trees that was barely visible and pointed his flashlight so that the beam of light shone on the narrow path. "I think this is where the owl is. Come on."

Chapter Two

Hardly any moonlight filtered through the dense pine branches.

"I don't know about this, Nate," said Vik.

"We'll be okay," said Nate. "I'll shine my light on the path so we can see our footing. You shine your flashlight up about fifteen feet off the ground. Sometimes owls nest in the fork of two branches. So look for lumps that might turn out to be owls."

It was slow going. The pools of light that Nate's flashlight made on the path showed dried leaves, rocks, twigs, and twisted tree roots. Suddenly, Nate stopped short. He knelt down and breathed. "Nice."

"What?" asked Vik.

Nate picked up an egg-shaped lump that looked like a big nut. "You know what this is?" he said. "It's an owl pellet."

"Owl pellet?" repeated Vik. "Sounds like a snack."

"You *could* eat one, I guess," said Nate. "But even you, Vacuum Vik, might not want to. Because I've got to tell you, owl pellets are little bundles of . . . well, like hardened throw up. The owl eats stuff like mice and other birds. The parts that the owl can't digest, it spits out in a pellet."

"Gross!" said Vik, impressed.

"Yeah," said Nate. He rolled the pellet on the palm of one hand. "You've got to soak a pellet before you can pull it apart and see what's in there. Usually, it's feathers and bones and skulls and stuff."

"Oh, man, you're making me hungry," joked Vik. "C'mon, let's find me my own owl pellet, and super size it with a side of fries."

But Nate wasn't listening. He was scanning the tree above with his flashlight. "Pellets are usually under an owl's nest," he said. "Do you see a nest up there?"

Vik beamed his flashlight on the tree. "Nope."

Nate walked forward on the path and saw that it skirted a ledge that dropped down to a darkened streambed. The first few days of camp had been rainy, but ever since then, the weather had been hot and dry, so the stream was just a trickle.

"Sure is dry," said Vik, walking ahead of Nate. "I'm . . . whoa!"

Nate looked over to see why Vik had stopped. A few inches from Vik's face hung a huge spiderweb across the trail, like a stop sign anchored in all directions with tight, shining thread. The delicate fibers caught the light from Vik's flashlight. In the middle of the web, a giant yellow spider—the size of a quarter, maybe even a silver dollar—froze in the light. Vik seemed frozen too. Then the spider and all of its eight legs skittered threateningly across the web, like a guard defending a treasure.

"Aaaaack!" Vik jumped back. The spider raced to the center of its web, standing its ground.

It might as well have been shaking a stick at Vik. "Let's get out of here," said Vik. He sounded genuinely scared. "That spider freaks me out."

"It's just—"Nate began.

But Vik cut him off. "Let's *go*," he said, and started off down another trail.

"Sure, okay," said Nate agreeably.

Vik set a brisk pace. After the boys had walked a while, Vik said, "Sorry we didn't find the owl."

"Hey, finding the pellet is nearly as good," said Nate. "I'll keep looking."

"You mean, *we'll* keep looking," Vik corrected him. "Count me in, 'cause except for the spider, it's been a ho-oo-ot."

"You got it," said Nate. He tucked the owl pellet in the pocket of his shorts. He'd have to soak the pellet for a while, but eventually he'd be able to pry it open and find out what was hiding inside. *Sort of like a time capsule,* he thought. He glanced at Vik. *Or a kid with a secret.*

Crunch, rustle, crunch, crunch, dried sticks cracked beneath their feet as Nate and Vik headed—

or thought they did, anyway—back to Birch Cabin.

★ ★ ★

Nate and Vik walked in silence for a while. Then Nate said, "I think we've gone too far."

"Yeah," agreed Vik. "So, like, are we lost in the woods in the middle of the night?"

"Not exactly. We just don't know where we are," Nate joked. "But don't sweat it. Just think that instead of a short cut, we're taking the *long* cut back to Birch."

A few minutes later, they were both glad when, through the trees, they could see the dusty, dry dirt road that led into camp.

"Don't ask me how we ended up *here*," said Nate. "I'm all turned around."

"I think it's my fault," said Vik. "I was so rattled that I led us in the wrong direction after we saw the spider."

"Well, the road'll lead us back now," said Nate. "No problem-o."

Just before they emerged from the woods

onto the road, Nate stopped.

"Wait!" he whispered.

"What?" said Vik. "Owl?"

"No," said Nate. "Over there on the road. I see someone."

"I see him too," said Vik. "It's probably Carlos or Simon looking for us."

"No, it's some guy I've never seen before," said Nate.

"Maybe it's a madman on the loose," said Vik. "Or, maybe it's the ghost of Camp Wolf Trail. Maybe it's . . . nah . . . let's just get out of here."

"Wait," said Nate again. He was curious.

The boys turned their flashlights off, stood behind a tree, and watched the man. He was older, tall and thin, and wore a cowboy hat. He held a cell phone to his ear. As he got closer, Nate and Vik could hear bits and pieces of his conversation.

"No, I'm up on the road," said the man. "There's no cell reception at the farm." He paused, and then sounding angry, he said, "I understand. But *you've* got to understand that now we're out of options. This could be the end for Herschel. Now he's probably done for."

What's that all about? thought Nate. *Whoever Herschel is, he's in trouble.*

Nate took a step back as the man walked past, heading away from camp. *Snap! Crack!* Nate stepped on a dry stick. The man turned his flashlight into the woods and shined it near the boys, searching for the source of the noise.

"Who's that?" the man asked.

Nate wasn't scared, just a little shaken. He was about to step forward and speak to the man, but Vik grabbed a handful of Nate's sweatshirt and held him back.

"No!" Vik hissed. "Run!"

Vik took off so Nate followed. Both boys clicked on their flashlights as they thrashed through the underbrush, with no idea where they were going. Beams from their flashlights bounced crazily on the ground and the low bushes that lined the path. Nate was fast, but Vik was faster. Vik's legs flew, his shoulders leaning forward, one hand out in front of him swatting at branches that grabbed at him. Even so, a thorny limb scratched Vik's face and Nate heard him yelp.

Nate was about to slow down. He wasn't even sure why they were running; the man wasn't chasing them. But then, *Ar-ooo!* A blood-curdling howl cut through the woods.

Nate gasped. He heard something behind him. It wasn't the man. This thing had four legs. It sounded like a wild animal panting, chasing, and crashing through the woods, hot on the boys' trail. Was it a bobcat? A bear? A wolf? Now Nate *was* scared.

Vik looked over his shoulder.

"Don't look back," Nate panted. "Just run!"

Nate's heart practically pounded out of his chest. Wildly, he scrambled through briars clawing at his shirt. He didn't look back. The panting and crashing kept coming. Closer, closer . . .

Finally, miraculously, Nate saw that Vik was leading him toward the faint glow of the battery-powered lantern that hung outside Birch Cabin. He and Vik threw themselves up the stairs, dove through the door, and landed in a heap on the floor, huffing and puffing, as the door slammed shut behind them.

Their seven cabin mates sat bolt upright in their sleeping bags. Someone shouted, "What's going on? What's—"

Then the door burst open *again*. A wild, hairy, flailing creature flung itself full speed at Nate and Vik.

Aroo, it howled. *Ar—ooooo!*

Chapter Three

Instantly, seven flashlights pointed light at Nate and Vik and whatever it was that was attacking them. In a nanosecond, everybody shouted, "Cookie!"

Cookie, the camp dog, smiled a drooly doggie smile and slurped Nate right on the face.

"Cookie?" Nate laughed, breathless. "It was you?"

"Aw, man," said Vik, shaking his head. "Talk about embarrassing." Vik's face was scraped, and the arm of his sweatshirt was stained with blood because he'd wiped his face on his sleeve, but he was laughing too. "Cookie the *dog* was the scary monster chasing us!"

All the guys laughed. Nate thought that they might poke fun at him and Vik a little bit, but instead, Zack said, "Hey, don't feel bad. Don't you remember? Cookie pulled that same stunt on Jim and me."

"Yeah," said Jim. "When Cookie chased us, I thought for sure the famous Wolf Trail wolf was on our tail. I was like, 'Run for your life!'"

Arf! Cookie barked, sounding proud of himself.

"Where were you guys, anyway?" Yasu asked Nate and Vik. "Did it take you this long to put out the fire?"

"Nah," said Vik.

Nate tensed. Would Vik tell everybody about the owl hunt? Nate wasn't really ready to go public about his interest in birds yet.

But Vik only said, "We were kind of on a wild goose chase."

Nate relaxed.

Vik went on, making the whole misadventure sound funny by poking fun at himself. "I freaked out when I heard Cookie-the-Killer-Dog chasing us," he said, "and before *that,* I freaked out when we heard a mystery man talking on his cell phone. And before *that*, I freaked out when I saw a spider." Vik flapped his hands and comically imitated himself, "Aaaaaccck! Help! A big, mean spider!"

As the guys laughed at Vik's exaggerated imitation of himself, Nate thought, *So being scared of spiders is* not *Vik's secret. It must be something else.*

"I was a mess," said Vik. "But not Nate. Talk about cool under pressure. He's not scared of *anything.*"

"Oh, yeah, right," said Nate. "Except I sure was scared of Ferocious Cookie." He nodded his head toward the dog, who had already fallen asleep and was snoring. "No prizes for smarts or bravery for me tonight, I guess."

"That's where you're wrong," said Jim. He hauled out from under his bunk a huge care package full of junk food. "I've got prizes for *everybody* tonight."

"Yahoo!" hollered all the campers. They

stampeded over to Jim's bunk to sort through his stash.

"Bad news, guys," joked Zack. "My trusty wilderness book, *The Outdoor Adventure Guide*, says that candy in the cabin will attract wild animals. This cabin will be an all-night diner to animals not so cute as Cookie over here. So we have a choice. We can either make Nate, who Vik says is not afraid of anything, lie by the door and guard us from The Attack of the Critters. Or, we've got to eat all of Jim's stuff tonight, right now."

"Let's eat!" hollered the boys.

"No one goes to sleep until every chocolate-covered peanut, gummy worm, and bag of Mammoth Munch has been eaten," said Jim.

"You got it!" cheered all the guys.

"Watch this!" said Zee. He dangled a green gummy worm above his own mouth and made it jiggle before he dropped it in.

Inspired, Kareem began to sing:
Great green globs of greasy grimy gopher guts . . .
Vik laughed. He sprang up and pulled a tennis

racket out from under his bunk. He yanked off its cover then strummed the strings as if the tennis racket were a guitar and he was providing music to go with Kareem's song.

After the boys had hollered out the last line—*And I forgot my spoon*—Jim nodded toward Vik's tennis racket.

"That's the first time you've used that thing," he said.

"What is it, a giant fly swatter?" joked Zee.

Vik quickly joked, "No, it's a spider swatter." He swung the racket crazily, as if he were fighting off a swarm of spiders. "You know me: Vik the Spider Chicken."

"Well, why'd you bring your tennis racket if you never use it?" asked Erik.

"Why'd you bring your toothbrush, Erik?" teased Yasu. "*You* never use *it*."

Not at all offended, Erik stuck a blue gummy worm across his top front teeth.

"Is that what that little brush is for?" he asked, pretending to be surprised. "I thought it was just a weird hair brush."

Yasu threw his pillow at Erik and soon the cabin was full of flying pillows.

It wasn't until later, when he was falling asleep, that Nate ran through the questions the night had brought up: *Where is that owl? Who is that mystery man? Who's Herschel? And what kind of trouble is Herschel in?*

★ ★ ★

Nate woke up the next morning to the slow *scritch, scritch, scritch* of branches scratching Birch Cabin's shingled roof—the side of it that wasn't covered with spongy, green moss. An early morning breeze carried a pine scent through the air. The scent almost overcame the sweaty-T-shirt-and-old-sneaker smell of Birch Cabin, which today had the added aroma of dog breath. That was thanks to Cookie, who'd spent the night on the floor.

Nate sighed happily. He never felt anything but content when he woke up in Birch Cabin. Like all the others, Birch Cabin was set out in the woods by itself. Soft summer light snuck in through the ivy that covered the old screens. Untouched tubes of toothpaste and half-full bottles of sunscreen lined a shelf. Trunks of various colors and sizes lined the walls; they were open and spilling out shoes, sweatshirts, and backpacks, mixed in with wet towels, swim trunks, a few books, and a lot of candy wrappers. On top of the heap on the floor lay a furry, snoring beast.

"Cookie," Nate whispered.

Cookie opened one eye.

Nate—his hair a fuzzy mess of bed-head—and Cookie were the only two awake in the cabin.

"Hey, buddy," whispered Nate. "Still tired

from making Vik and me look like doofuses last night?"

Without moving his head, the dog turned his big brown eyes toward Nate. Cookie exhaled, as if to say, "Huh! That was easy!"

Nate looked around. There was Jim, his long legs sticking out the end of his bunk, and Erik, who was quiet only because he was asleep. Yasu and Zee were just lumps in their sleeping bags. Kareem, a first-year camper, slept in a Camp Wolf Trail T-shirt he'd inherited from his dad, who'd come to camp twenty-five years ago. Sean, another newbie, was wearing his swim trunks.

Then there was Vik, the scrapes and cuts on his cheek scabbed over. *Not too bad, but still. Ouch. His face.* Nate grimaced with sympathy.

Careful not to make noise, Nate slipped off his top bunk and dropped to his feet. He tiptoed around the dog and the crinkly candy wrappers that littered the floor, eased his notebook and pencil out of the back pocket of the shorts he'd worn the day before, and swung himself back up to his bunk.

He opened his notebook to a clean page and admired its potential. What would he draw or write this morning? He used to keep the notebook just for jotting down the names of the birds he'd seen. But over the winter, his grandfather had given him a book about drawing birds. Now the pages of his notebook included sketches of birds and bird parts. Sometimes he made notes about what the birds did or where he'd seen them, and lots of times, he wrote questions to ask himself.

I didn't get to see that owl, thought Nate. *But I could draw what I think it might look like.*

He picked up his pencil and drew two circles for the owl's eyes, a circle for the head, and an oval for the body. He filled in details with feathery strokes of the pencil and drew a branch for a perch. He wished he had his colored pencils from home to make golden rings that would be the owl's eyes; he kind of liked to do things right.

Cookie heaved himself up and shook, sending dog hair and bits of dust flying through the air. The dog glanced up at Nate as if to say, "I'm outta here." Cookie stretched, then walked toward the door. He nudged it open with his nose and slipped out.

Slam! The door swung shut behind him.

At the noise, the other Birch Cabiners started to stretch and roll in their beds.

Quickly, Nate dusted eraser crumbs off of his unfinished owl sketch and wrote the date. Under that, he scrawled:

Saw a huge spider.
No owl, but pellet. Where is that owl?

Nate closed his notebook, shoved the pencil back into the spiral wire, and tucked it under his pillow, thinking no one had noticed.

But Jim had. "Oh, good idea," he said to Nate. "Writing, I mean. If I don't write home soon, my family'll come up here and make me."

Vik sat up and shot Nate a look that said,

Phew, that was a close one. He knew that Nate didn't want everyone to know that he wrote about birds in his notebook.

"Yowser!" said Sean, looking at Vik's face. "Nice war wounds. Are you okay?"

"Yeah," said Vik. "My face hurts a little."

"It's killing me!" joked Yasu.

"I've got one word for you people," said Zee, already in his swim trunks. "And it's *mana-plungee*! Word-of-the-day. It means, *Let's go*."

"Mana-plungee!" Books and pillows fell to the floor as the boys jumped off their bunks yelling, "Mana-plungee! Mana-plungee!"

They yanked on their swim trunks, sprinted out of the cabin, then ran full-tilt, yipping and screaming "Mana-plungee" as they careened down the path to the lake, kicking up dust the whole way.

Chapter Four

Of course, the boys couldn't go swimming without a counselor present. But luckily, Simon was an early riser and on waterfront duty already. There he was, his whistle strung around his neck, sitting in a wobbling, grungy lawn chair. He was reading a thick book, his legs propped up on a rock.

"You guys are insane," Simon shouted, jumping up from his chair as the boys stampeded toward him. "I love it!" He stuck a twig in his book for a bookmark. "Buddy-up!" he ordered. "Flip your tags on the pegboard. And *nooooo*-body jumps in till I say so."

In pairs, the boys went to the pegboard to turn

their tags from green to red. Then they padded out to the end of dock, their bare feet *slap, slap, slapping* on the smooth wood, and waited. They all knew Simon was a total stickler for safety. After the last pair of boys had checked in, Simon grabbed the foam rescue tube, then walked out to the end of the dock, standing with his feet apart in lifeguard stance. "Ready," said Simon. "Go!"

"Mana-plungee! Ya-*hoo*!" The boys cannon-balled, dove, belly-flopped, jumped, flipped, and jack-knifed off the dock into the morning-cold water. Nate held his breath, anticipating the shock. He rose up on his toes, pushed off, and sliced into the water in a perfect dive. At the same time his swim buddy, Sean, fell backward into the water hollering, "Mana-plungee!"

"Splash fight!" yelled Erik. Wildly, the boys swatted the water to make it splash up, or kicked so hard with their legs that pretty soon it seemed surprising to Nate that there was any water left in the lake at all. And all the while, the boys were making a deafening racket, howling and yowling

as loud as they could. Nate wondered if Simon would tell them to stop. He didn't, but Nate did notice that they had scared away a few geese that took off honking and squawking and flapping their huge wings. *I'd like to sketch those geese in flight,* Nate thought. Then he asked himself two questions: *I wonder if they've got a nest nearby?* Nate grinned to himself. *And I wonder if Vik'll be up for a* real *wild goose chase later?*

When they were tired of splashing, the guys swam out to the old wooden floating raft anchored partway out in the lake for round after round of jumping in, swimming around, climbing back on, and jumping in again. After a while, as if they all understood each other's thoughts, the boys headed back toward the main dock.

"The water feels so warm now," said Zack, breathing hard after his swim back to the dock. "Warmer than the air."

Nate hated to get out of the water. But his stomach growled. Breakfast! A morning plunge had a way of making a camper extra-hungry. Nate danced a little jig to shake off the dripping water. The rest of the boys followed. They hopped and shook like dogs, pushing each other and laughing. They turned their tags on the pegboard from red to green and picked up their towels to dry themselves off.

Just then, the clunky jangle of the breakfast bell clanged.

"See ya, Simon!" said Jim, as the parade to the dining hall began.

"No way! I'm coming to breakfast with you guys," Simon said. "Otherwise, all the food'll be gone by the time I get there. Just coffee grinds and orange rinds'll be left."

Yasu moaned, "I'm so hungry right now, I could eat a horse."

"Careful there, Yasu," said Simon, as they walked along. "I wouldn't talk about eating a horse if I were you."

"How come?" asked Yasu.

"Spoiler alert," said Simon. "Pretty soon, a horse may be your best buddy."

"Say *what*?" asked Yasu.

"You're going to be *riding* a horse," said Simon.

"Do *what*?" asked Yasu.

"Riding a horse," said Simon. "You know: Giddy-yup, Whoa, Neigh. The whole deal. Isabels go on a horse trek in a few days."

Yasu whooped cowboy-style, "Yee, dogies! All right, Isabels!"

The Isabels were a cluster, a group made up of campers of various ages who went on outings together, did chores together, and teamed up on theme days. This year, every cluster was named after the punch line of a knock-knock joke. Vik, Nate, Zee, and Yasu were in "Isabel Necessary on a Bike?" They were known as the Isabels, for short. Jim, Zack, Erik, Kareem, and Sean were in the cluster called "Orange You Glad I Didn't Say Banana?" They were known as the Orange You Glads.

"Isabels get to go horseback riding?" Kareem said. "And Orange You Glads don't? That is so not fair!"

"Don't worry," said Simon. "You Orange You Glads will have a turn to ride. Meanwhile, it'll be your turn to do Oddball Championships while the Isabels are gone."

The Oddball Championships were a Camp Wolf Trail tradition. Campers invented wacky games and contests—like The Go-Nowhere Canoe Race, in which the *last* canoe won; or the Weird Tennis Ball Contraption, won by the craziest non-mechanical machine set in motion by a tennis ball. *Everybody* loved the Oddballs!

"The Orange You Glads will do Oddball Championships?" said Kareem. "That's all right then."

By now the spicy smell of sausage prickled everybody's noses, and the boys tromped and stomped up the path to the dining hall, beating out the rhythm and singing to the tune of "We Will, We Will Rock You":

We want,
We want,
BreakFAST.

"Hope you're hungry, boys," hollered Skeeter Malone, the camp chef, as he ushered them into the dining hall. "We've got sausage, pancakes and warm maple syrup, scrambled eggs, bacon, orange juice—"

"Orange juice?" cheered Jim. "Orange Juice Glad? Orange Juice Glad rules!"   Zack, Erik, Kareem, and Sean cheered too.

Nate laughed, but then his mind slipped back to horses. *I've never been anywhere near a horse before*, he thought, *and now we're going on a horseback trek*. Then in his typical way, Nate asked himself a question: *How hard could horseback riding really be?*

Nate often thought that the birds must like Camp Wolf Trail a lot better when there were no campers around, when the only sounds were the whispering of the trees in the breeze, the slosh of the lake water against the dock, and maybe once in a while, the croak of a bullfrog. But oh, man! When the campers were at camp, it was really noisy: yelling, talking, clinking, clanging, pounding, slamming, shouting, and chanting. And *that* was all in the dining hall! Every once in a while, some guy or group of guys got up and sang a camp song, or a song they'd made up. Like right now, a kid named Nico was standing on a table, leading the other kids from Spruce Cabin in singing to the tune of "Roll Out the Barrel":

> *Roll out the breakfast,*
> *We'll drink an ocean of juice,*
> *Ten million pancakes,*
> *We're champs at eating:*
> *We're Spruce!!!*

Then, as Nico formed the letters using his body and arms and legs, everybody shouted: "*S-P-R-U-C-E!* Spruce, Spruce, Spruce! Hooray!"

Nico went airborne, jumping off the table and onto the floor. Nate cheered till he was hoarse, along with everyone else. At home and at school, Nate was constantly being told to be quiet. One of the many things he loved about Camp Wolf Trail was that here, the louder the better. *Sorry, birds,* Nate thought.

The campers dug in and devoured plates piled high with eggs and bacon, toast and pancakes. Most of the boys were still eating when one of the counselors from Pawpaw Cabin began yelling out the announcements.

"Listen up!" he said. "We've had no rain in a while, so we've gotta save water. No showers. Get clean swimming."

"Yahoo!" hollered the boys.

"What's a shower?" yelled one joker. "Never heard of it!"

The counselor went on: "Isabels, meet here after breakfast." Then he held up an empty juice pitcher and asked, "Whadda-yuh say?"

Every single kid shouted, "You kill it, you fill it."

That was one of the Camp Wolf Trail rules: Whoever used the last of something refilled it.

After breakfast, when most of the rest of the campers had filed out of the dining hall, the Isabels gathered at one table. In addition to the Isabels in Birch Cabin—Vik, Nate, Yasu, and Zee—there

were two older Isabels—Nico and Wu-Tsing—
and Tyler and Will, who were the same age as the
Birch Cabiners.

"Scootch over, please," said Simon, slipping
onto the bench. Nate moved over. "Thanks," said
Simon. "Okay, so—"

Poing. A flying fork interrupted Simon. It
flew over Nate's shoulder and landed with a clang
on the table in front of him.

"Sorry about that! Fork Game," explained
one of the campers lingering at the table behind
them. Fork Game involved hitting the tongs of a
fork with your fist. The goal was to flip the fork
into an empty water pitcher.

Without missing a beat, Simon picked the fork up and tossed it back over Nate's head. "Anyway, dudes," said Simon, "I've got some news. The counselors did a coin toss at the meeting last night and it turns out that the Isabels are going to be the first to have a horse adventure. It'll be an overnight pack trip."

The Isabels pounded the table, whooping and whistling so loudly that Nate thought the noise would bring down the roof of the dining hall.

"I'm going too," said Simon. "I grew up with horses. My mom teaches kids to ride."

"Seriously?" said Nico. "Wow."

"Yeah, I've been riding since I was a baby. My mom used to strap me into this little saddle and off we'd go," said Simon, lurching from side to side, pretending to be a baby on a horse. The boys laughed, imagining a baby Simon strapped into a saddle on a big beast of a horse.

"Did you ever get kicked or bitten or fall off?" asked Tyler.

"All of the above," said Simon. "Still do,

from time to time."

"Cool," said Tyler, sounding as though he meant the exact opposite.

But Zee seemed enthusiastic. "This is going to be so awesome," he said. "We can race the horses, and gallop, and jump."

"Oh, yeah?" said Nico. He smiled and pointed his thumb at Zee and said to the rest of the guys: "Yo, get a load of the Lone Ranger over here."

"Not exactly," said Zee, smiling, "but my mom's friend has a horse. So I've ridden before."

"All right, guys," said Simon. "Is there anyone who doesn't want to go?" He paused. When no one spoke up, Simon continued: "Okay! Here's the scoop. We've partnered with a horse rescue organization that's renting an old farm nearby. Starting this morning, you guys will work with the horses and get to know them for a couple of days, and then we'll head out on the overnight trip. The man in charge of the horses is named Joe. He'll run the show."

Wu-Tsing straddled the bench as if it were

a saddle and comically pretended to swing a lasso. "Hee-haw!" he yodeled.

Zee began to sing a cowboy song: "Whoopee tie yie yo, git along, little dogies!"

When no one else knew his song, Zee switched to "Home on the Range." He and the other Isabels sang:

Home, home on the range,
Where the deer and the antelope play . . .

"Suit up, cowpokes," said Simon, loudly. "You'll need to put on long pants and shoes."

"Shoes?" groaned the boys. None of them had worn shoes much since they'd arrived at camp.

Simon shrugged. "Okay, wear flip-flops and see how well that's working for you when your feet are in stirrups, or you're stepping in horse poop," he said. "Meet me back here in five minutes, and we'll go to the farm."

Chapter Five

It took longer than five minutes for the boys to return. Zee couldn't find any long pants so he had to borrow a pair from Vik, and Yasu had taken the laces out of his high-top sneakers to use as a make-shift fishing line, so he had to loop them back into his high-tops. But finally the boys all gathered and met up with Tyler and Will and the older guys, Nico and Wu-Tsing. They were all wearing long pants and real shoes.

Simon led the boys along the path to the farm. After a few minutes of walking, the path led up to an open field. Part of the field was a paddock, surrounded by a weather-beaten fence. The posts of the fence listed left and right and the fence boards buckled and sagged. Buckets hung from eye hooks on some of the posts. Just outside the fence, there was a simple wooden shed with bales of hay next to it.

Eight horses stood in the paddock, sunning themselves.

"Soooo," breathed Nico. "There they are."

"Cool!" said Will.

The boys walked toward the fence, following a mowed path through the tall, dry, scratchy grass. The field smelled like hay and buzzed with flying grasshoppers and unidentified chirping insects.

"Those horses are huge!" said Yasu as the group approached the paddock.

Nate agreed, though he said nothing. He stood away from the fence.

The dusty horses seemed hot and uninterested in meeting the boys. They swished their tails in each other's faces and pulled up great mouthfuls of grass, which they chewed noisily.

Yasu leaned over a fallen-down part of the

fence. "Here horsey, horsey," he called, stretching out his hand.

"You don't do it like that," said Zee. He reached down, grabbed a bunch of grass, and held it out to a gray horse. The horse snorted dismissively and walked off.

"I guess you don't do it like *that*, either," said Wu-Tsing.

"Why do you think they keep stamping their feet?" asked Will.

"Hooves, not feet," said Nico.

"It's just to keep the flies away," said Simon. "That's why they twitch their skin, and swish their tails around too."

The boys—except for Nate—reached over the fence, calling to entice the horses to come over. But the horses startled at the boys' loud voices, and moved away.

"I think we need a rope to lasso them," said Wu-Tsing. "Loop it up, toss it over the horse's neck, and—"

"All you need to do is be quiet," said Simon.

"The horses will come over when they're good and ready."

Simon was right. As the boys waited silently, a brown, black, and white splotched horse walked toward them and lifted her head over the fence. The faded blue halter she wore on her head had a fresh piece of tape with the name CHRISTMAS WISH written on it in bright permanent ink.

"She's a pinto," said Simon, patting her neck. "That means a horse with a spotted pattern."

There were eight horses in all. In addition to Christmas Wish, there were three reddish-colored horses, one of which had white patches. There were two gray horses, one dark brown horse with a bushy mane and tail, and one skinny brown horse.

Vik joined Nate, who was still standing a foot or so away from the fence. "Whaddya think of our four-legged friends here?" asked Vik.

"Well," said Nate, "except for being different colors, the horses all look about the same to me: two twitchy ears, two giant eyes, lots of giant yellow teeth, one tail, and really bad haircuts, mane-wise."

"I thought for sure *that* horse would be your favorite," said Vik, with a grin. He pointed to the skinny brown horse over in the corner of the paddock standing in the only strip of shade that was provided by the shed.

Nate looked. The brown horse looked like a bag of bones. It hung its head, and its shoulder bones stuck up sharply under its dull coat. Its haunches were sharp, too, sticking up from its rump. Along its narrow back, Nate noticed a pair of small brown birds sitting as if they had not a care in the world. So *that's* why Vik thought he'd like the brown horse.

"Those are cowbirds," Nate told Vik. "They don't mind the horse, and the horse doesn't mind them."

"That horse is too spaced out to mind much of anything," said Vik.

"Okay, guys, listen up," said Simon.

Nate and Vik looked at Simon, turning their backs to the fence as they listened to him explain that Joe, the horse guy, would meet them at the

paddock soon.

Suddenly, Nate heard a long, loud sigh and felt hot, damp breath exhaled on the back of his neck.

"Yow!" yelped Nate as he jumped in the air. "What was that?"

He turned and came face-to-muzzle with the bony brown horse, who'd stretched his neck out over the fence. The horse's splotchy nostrils were covered with dust. His eyes were runny, as if he was crying, and he had a long, stringy mane. The cowbirds had flown off his back, but a few flies rested on his face. The horse looked at Nate and blew another warm, wet gust of a greeting. Nate could see the pink inside of his droopy lower lip. To Nate, it seemed like a whale had just blasted him with spray from his blowhole.

"Thanks a lot, horse," said Nate as he wiped horse breath off his face. The horse was close enough that Nate could see a name on a dirty old piece of tape on the halter. Nate could barely make out the faded letters, which spelled HERSCHEL.

Vik shot Nate a look and said, "Herschel?"

Where have I heard that name before? Nate thought.

"Look at that lip," Yasu was saying, pointing to Herschel. "It hangs to his knees!"

"I hope I don't have to ride *him*," said Zee. "He's a real mutt."

Nate suddenly remembered why the name sounded familiar, and he knew that Vik did too: *The man who Vik and I saw in the woods was talking about Herschel. So it turns out that Herschel's not a person; he's a horse.* Nate also remembered that the man had said that Herschel was probably done for. *Done for? What does that mean?* Nate looked at Herschel, and Herschel returned his gaze squarely. *This horse doesn't look like much, but Vik's wrong about him. There's a brain in there, and it's a sharp one.*

Nate thought about how sometimes the plainest birds used their plainness in deceptive ways, like a wren who would fluff out its dirt-brown feathers to camouflage itself and outsmart a hungry hawk. Nate wondered, *Would I be wrong to judge* you *by* your *appearance, Herschel?* Just then, a rattling, rusty white pickup truck pulled up next to the shed. The horses bobbed their heads, pricked their ears, and looked at the truck as if it were an old buddy. Nate saw a tall, skinny man with a cowboy hat climb out of the truck.

"Hi, Simon. Hi, boys," the man said as he walked toward them. His voice was gravelly but friendly. "I'm Joe. Y'all ready to earn your lunch?"

Vik nudged Nate, and Nate nodded. The instant they heard his voice, they both realized that Joe was the man on his cell phone, talking about Herschel during their owl adventure.

"This guy's my madman?" whispered Vik. "The one I ran away from? He's about as scary as Cookie."

The horses sure seemed to think Joe was a nice guy. They didn't take their eyes off him and jostled each other out of the way to be near him. One horse rubbed his forehead on Joe's back as if he were scratching a post. Another horse snuffled Joe's pockets for treats.

Nate's mind was a stew of questions. *Why had Joe sounded so angry on the phone that night? What had he meant when he'd said that Herschel was out of options? Was Herschel the horse sick or dying or vicious or something? Was Joe as nice as he seemed now, or was he as scary and tough as he'd sounded before?*

"So, who's ridden before?" Joe asked.

Zee, Nico, and Tyler raised their hands.

Joe nodded. "Okay, good," he said. The sound of his voice seemed to soothe the horses. Joe went on: "The most important thing to remember around horses is safety. Don't make loud noises. Don't run around. And, when you're working with a horse, always make sure the horse knows where you are. They like it if you talk to them."

"What do you say to them?" asked Yasu.

"How about: 'Why the long face?'" Vik joked. The rest of the boys groaned.

But Joe smiled. "You can say pretty much anything you want. And if you listen closely, you can understand what the horse says back. A horse'll never lie to you."

Just then one of the red horses lifted her head and whinnied.

"What's *she* saying?" asked Wu-Tsing.

"I think she's hungry," said Simon.

"You're right, Simon," said Joe. He grinned at the campers, saying, "You guys can help me feed the horses this morning. Put a half scoop of grain in each one of those buckets hanging on the fence." He nodded toward Nico and Wu-Tsing and said, "You older boys, see that hay over there? You can spread it out. Try not to waste any; we've got a lot of hungry mouths to feed."

As soon as the boys headed toward the food, a horse knocked at the fence with a hoof as if to say, "Hurry up!" Nate noticed that the horses had the same hungry look that Cookie did every time there was food around. Tyler and Zee helped Nate dump the sweet-smelling grain into the wheelbarrow.

Some of the horses began to stamp and nicker with impatience.

"We're coming, we're coming!" said Vik as he pushed the grain wheelbarrow over to the buckets hanging on the fence.

Tyler filled the scoop halfway, then reached inside the fence boards to dump the grain into a bucket. The red horse stepped forward and stuffed her nose into the bucket, snuffling and slurping the feed. Tyler filled the next bucket, and the next, and two more horses stepped up to eat.

Tyler handed the scoop to Nate.

"Batter up," he said. "Want a turn?"

Nate actually *didn't*. It was weird and surprising: being close to the horses made him uncomfortable. But he shook it off and said, "Uh, okay." He dug the scoop into the soft pile of sticky grain and reached through the fence to fill the next empty bucket. Just as he did, a gray horse stuffed her head in the bucket sliming Nate's hand. Startled, Nate lurched away and dropped the scoop. It clunked against the bucket and fell to the ground. The horse threw up her head and pitched backward, knocking the bucket off its hook and spilling grain onto the ground.

Nate felt embarrassed when Simon said, "That horse won't hurt you, Nate. She just wants her breakfast." Simon reached through the fence and rehung the bucket on its hook. Then he picked up the scoop and offered it to Nate. Nate hesitated.

Quickly, Vik took the scoop from Simon, saying, "Can I do it now?"

"Sure thing," said Simon.

As Vik refilled the gray horse's bucket, Nate noticed Herschel was looking right at him. *So, are you sizing me up, Herschel?* Nate thought. *Can you tell that I am uncomfortable?* Herschel shifted his gaze to Vik as Vik filled Herschel's feed bucket with grain. Herschel pointed his ears toward Vik with a hopeful look.

"You are one skinny horse, Herschel," said Vik. He scooped a little extra feed for Herschel.

"Doesn't anyone ever feed you? C'mon you bag of bones. Here's your food."

The horse plodded toward the bucket. Nate watched him eat. The other horses had gobbled their food. Not Herschel. Herschel lifted his head out of the bucket now and then, grain drizzling out of the sides of his mouth with every slow chew.

"You're a good boy, Herschel, " Vik said as he patted the horse's neck. "Even if you are a mess."

Chapter Six

"Hey," Nate said to Vik, when no one could hear him. "Thanks for taking over with the feeding. I don't know why, but being close to these horses gives me the heebie-jeebies."

"Like me and the spider," said Vik.

"I guess," said Nate. He felt sheepish, especially after Vik had praised him for being brave after the owl hunt. "You're doing great with the horses, though."

"Yeah, I'm surprised. I didn't think I would," admitted Vik. "Especially when I first saw them. I mean, horses are so much bigger in real life than you think they're going to be, and they smell so much worse!"

Nate laughed.

Vik continued: "I especially like old Herschel here. I was wrong about him. He's not stupid. He's just laid-back. What do you think Joe meant when he said Herschel was done for?"

Nate shook his head. "No idea," he said. He reached out tentatively to pat Herschel's neck, then changed his mind and stuck his hand in his back pocket, next to his bird notebook. "What's the matter with me?" he muttered under his breath, disgusted at the discovery he'd made about himself. "Why am I scared of a horse?"

"Hey, don't sweat it," said Vik. "You'll get used to these horses, even Herschel. He's ugly, but that's part of his charm. Right, Herschel?"

Herschel snorted, but in a friendly way.

"Okay, everybody," Joe said. "Next thing on your list is the water trough. Empty it, scrub it out, rinse it with water from the hose, dump that water out, and fill it with fresh water."

"Be careful," said Simon. "Don't waste the water. Remember, we're having a dry spell."

"I get the hose!" said Will.

"I call the sponge!" said Zee and Yasu at the same time.

When the boys shouted and ran to get the hose and the sponges, all of the horses startled at the commotion—all except for Herschel. The horses left their buckets and rushed to the other end of the paddock.

"See what I mean?" said Joe. "They spook easy."

Birds spook easy too, thought Nate. *Maybe horses and birds aren't so different. So how come the horses spook me?*

"What about that horse?" asked Zee, pointing to Herschel, who hadn't left his bucket.

"Herschel is a really smart horse," said Joe. "He's an old, experienced kind of guy. A steady Eddie."

After the boys had been quiet for a few seconds, the other horses came back. Trying to move slowly and carefully, the boys set to work scrubbing out the water trough.

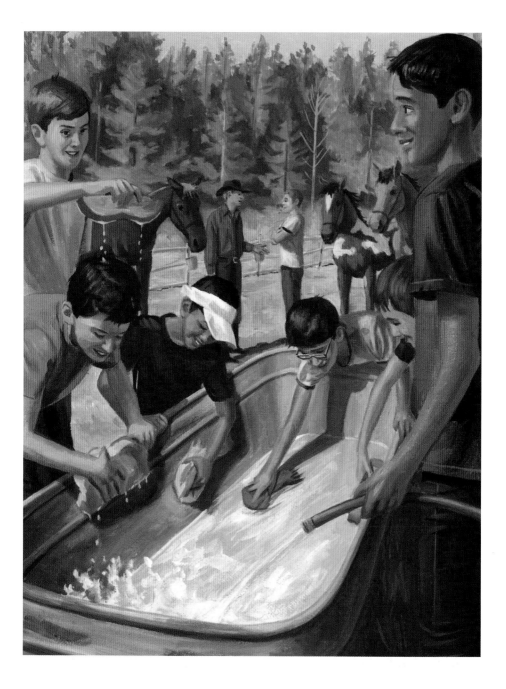

"Are all of these horses yours, Joe?" asked Nate.

"No," said Joe. "My horse, April, is back at my house. These other horses here, I'm taking care of temporarily, while I try to find them homes."

"So, who owns them?" asked Nico.

"Nobody, yet," said Joe. "These horses were all homeless for one reason or another. I run a horse rescue operation. People who can't take care of their horses anymore give them to me, and I buy horses at auctions that no one else wants. I met your camp director last winter and we came up with a plan to have you Wolf Trail campers work with the horses. Good for the boys, good for the horses."

"Where did Christmas Wish come from?" asked Zee.

"Family up the road," said Joe. "Had to move and couldn't keep her. She's pretty. She's sure to get adopted soon. And the chestnuts—those are the reddish ones—will get a home before Labor Day, that's what I predict. The gray horses I found at an auction, which can be a really bad place for horses. But the grays are in good shape, and so's the big bay. That's the brown one with the black legs. Somebody will come along and adopt them."

"What about Herschel?" asked Vik.

"Well, I thought I'd found him a home, but the folks just changed their minds," said Joe. He shook his head. "Herschel's not much to look at. He's not young. He's not sleek. So far, nobody wants him."

Nate and Vik didn't even need to look at one another. Now they understood what they'd overheard Joe saying on his cell phone. He must have been talking to the people who'd changed their minds about wanting Herschel. Everyone looked at Herschel, who had gone back to the corner of the paddock. Joe went on: "Herschel was at that same auction as the grays. He was for sale with a bunch of other scared, homeless horses. I took Herschel and the grays because I didn't want them to get sold for meat."

"Meat?" a few boys asked, all at the same time.

"Yeah, meat," said Joe. "For exotic animals, even for people in other countries to eat." Joe stuffed his hands in his pockets and kicked the fence. His voice sounded angry again, the way it had when he was talking on his cell phone. "Bad things can happen to unwanted horses."

"But someone *will* adopt Herschel eventually, right?" asked Nico.

"Who knows?" said Joe. "So far, it's not looking good."

All the boys were quiet.

"Hey, but there's still hope," said Joe. He settled his hat on his head and spoke cheerfully, saying, "Okay, boys. Thanks for your help. You better hightail it over to the dining hall for lunch now. I'll see you tomorrow morning bright and early."

As Simon walked the boys back to camp, Zee tried to lift their spirits by leading them in singing another one of his cowboy songs:

Happy trails to you
Until we meet again.
Happy trails to you
Keep smiling until then.

Nate looked over his shoulder at Herschel, thinking, *Will there by happy trails for you, Herschel?*

The old horse pawed at the ground with one hoof, raising a small sad cloud of dust.

★ ★ ★

That night, in his bunk with his covers pulled up over his head and his flashlight on, Nate sketched two little brown-headed cowbirds in his notebook. Then he wrote:

Cowbirds like horses. why don't I?

Chapter Seven

Nate woke to the chatter of a very talkative cardinal. He flopped onto his stomach so that he could look out the screen and he caught a fleeting glimpse of bright red flash as the cardinal flew away. *Wish I had my colored pencils with me,* Nate thought. *I'd sketch that cardinal just as a streak of red.* For some reason, Nate always thought of cardinals as signs of good luck. *And I'll need good luck today,* he thought, with a twist of dread in his stomach. *Today, I have to ride a horse.*

After breakfast, Nate and the other Isabels walked down the dusty dirt path to the paddock for their first riding lesson. Nate's jeans felt stiff and heavy and hot. *Wearing nothing much else than a bathing suit for two weeks at camp is a much better way to go*, Nate thought. He sure did wish he was going swimming right *now*. The other guys were practically running toward the paddock, jostling one another out of the way to be the one to get there first. Yasu, as usual, was in the lead, and Nate brought up the rear, with Vik just ahead of him.

Joe and Simon had lined the horses up along the paddock fence. Now the two men moved among the horses, putting on saddles and adjusting the bridles on the horses' heads.

When he saw the boys, Joe said, "Morning, cowpokes! I've got helmets in the back of the truck. Find one that fits. When you're ready, come on over, and Simon or I will help you get on your horse."

"You okay?" Vik asked Nate as Joe rattled off the names of which boy would ride which horse.

"Uh, yeah," Nate said as he grinned a weak grin. "Sort of wish I hadn't had so much sausage for breakfast, though, or any breakfast at all, come to think of it."

Simon helped some of the boys get on their horses, and other boys stood on an old cement block and mounted their horses themselves.

"Vik," said Joe. "You're on Christmas Wish."

Nate watched as Vik stood on the cement block and then swung himself into the saddle as easily as if he'd done it every day of his life. Christmas Wish started to walk sideways, but Vik leaned forward, patted the horse's neck, and murmured calming words. Christmas Wish swiveled her ears back toward Vik and stood still.

"Son, you are a born horseman!" Joe said to Vik. "Okay, walk on over to the shade with Christmas Wish." Joe turned. "Nate, you're up next," he said. "I'm gonna put you on Herschel, okay?"

"Sure," said Nate, though he *wasn't* sure how he felt about this arrangement. But he supposed that if he was going to ride, he might as well be on Herschel, who didn't look capable of any fast, sudden movement. Slowly, Nate came and stood next to Herschel, who stood still as a statue, not even swishing his chewed-looking tail at flies.

"Lift your foot back," said Joe, showing Nate how to bend his leg.

Nate squared his shoulders and forced himself to push down his fear. *Do this*, he ordered himself.

Nate reached up and grabbed a kind of handle on the saddle, the pommel. Joe pushed him up and Nate swung his leg over Herschel. It wasn't pretty, but Nate landed—*plonk*—astride the saddle. Nate held on for dear life, but Herschel didn't move a muscle while Joe adjusted the stirrups. It was as if Herschel knew how uneasy Nate felt, and the horse wanted to help Nate get used to being way up there on his back.

"Take the reins, son," Joe said.

Nate held the reins, but he still held onto the pommel too. He sat as if he were frozen stiff. Man, the ground looked a long way off!

"Horses are big creatures," Joe said in a conversational tone as he refastened a buckle under Herschel's hairy chin. "It's smart to be aware of that. Makes you more careful, more respectful. Herschel here, he'll be a real gentleman for you if

you treat him politely."

Nate swallowed. He was grateful for Joe's reassurance, and he was grateful that Joe continued to stand next to Herschel and him as he instructed the boys.

"You have several ways to ask your horse to do what you want him to do," said Joe. "A squeeze with your legs—not a kick with your heels—asks him to move forward. A gentle pull on your reins asks him to move left or right. Pull back a bit to stop. Your voice can ask him to 'whoa.' When we're on the trail, these horses will just follow my horse. But for now, you're going to stay in the paddock and get to know each other."

Joe led Herschel forward and Nate held his breath, certain that he'd fall, crashing to the ground in a big *thunk*, looking like a total stooge.

But even though Herschel was bony, and knock-kneed, he had a surprisingly smooth walk; it was slow, easy, and comfortable. Once Nate got used to the way the saddle rocked a bit from side to side with every step, he began to breathe, though he sure didn't try to make Herschel trot, like some of the other boys did with their horses. Nor did he loosen his death grip on the pommel. Nate rode Herschel in circles around the paddock. He tried to imagine that he was a cowbird on Herschel's back. *But if I were, I'd take off and fly away and never look back,* he thought.

"Hey, man, look at you, *riding,*" said Vik, easing Christmas Wish to fall into step with Herschel, "Great, huh?"

"No," Nate corrected him, serious but grinning. "First of all, I'm not riding just any old horse. I'm riding *Herschel,* the world's *slowest* horse. And I'm still shaky about it."

"How come?" asked Vik.

"Ya got me," said Nate. "I mean, I'm big and smelly myself, with huge feet, so you'd think I wouldn't mind the horses. I think it's that they're unpredictable. That's what scares me."

"Well," Vik said, "the way I see it, it's easy to do stuff you're not scared of. Doing what you're scared of? That's brave."

"Thanks," said Nate. "And thanks for not telling all the other guys I'm a horse-a-phobe. Thanks for not blabbing about the birds, either."

"When're you going to be brave about *that*, and tell everybody about your bird notebook?" Vik asked.

"Not yet," said Nate. "Still chicken."

"A chicken's a bird, so I guess that's appropriate," said Vik. "But I gotta tell you, I think you're wrong about the guys. I don't think any of them would tease you about the horses *or* your bird notebook. But it's up to you to spill or not spill."

★ ★ ★

It seemed like forever, but really, it was only about an hour that the boys practiced asking their horses to walk forward and turn left and right, or turn in a half-circle to change direction. Nate was very glad when Joe told the boys to dismount. He was the first to slide off and put his two feet on the ground again. His legs felt wobbly.

"So?" Simon asked Nate. "Yesterday, you didn't even want to feed the horses, and today you're a rider. Whaddya say?"

"I'd say horseback riding is not my favorite activity," said Nate honestly. "But it definitely fits right in the category of things that eventually may *possibly* be not as totally terrible as I thought."

"Glad to hear it," said Simon. He thumped Nate on the shoulder.

Simon and Joe showed the boys how to take the saddles off and hose the horses down. Before heading back to camp, Nate reached through the fence to pat Herschel and this time, he didn't pull his hand back. Nate touched Herschel's warm, whiskery muzzle.

"Thanks, Herschel," Nate said.

All the boys were hot, thirsty, and tired as they walked back to camp.

"I'm as dried up as an old raisin," complained Tyler.

"My legs are so achy, I can hardly walk," said Wu-Tsing.

"*My* legs are so *bow-legged*, I can hardly walk," said Will.

Zee was the only one with enough energy to sing. And even he wasn't very loud as he sang:

I'm an old cowhand,
From the Rio Grande,
And I learned to ride
'fore I learned to stand . . .

Then Yasu came alive. "Who's for a plunge in oh-man-it's cold O'Mannitt's Cove?" he hollered, naming a part of Evergreen Lake where the water never warmed up. Without waiting for an answer, Yasu started to jog so that he'd be the first one back to the cabin to change into swim trunks, and the first one into the lake. The rest were close behind.

Later, when Nate dove into the smooth, cool water under the watchful eye of Simon, and the water washed away the dust and smell of sweat-encrusted, sun-baked horse-hair, Nate felt relieved. No more horseback riding—at least not today!

And he could face it tomorrow, as long as he was facing it with Herschel.

★ ★ ★

"Guys, wake up. Wake up!" Carlos yelled as he stood in the middle of Birch Cabin in the middle of the night.

"What? What's going on?" Jim asked as he disentangled himself from his sheets and flicked on his flashlight. Zack sat up in his top bunk so quickly that he practically bonked his head on a beam, and Kareem rolled over and fell off his bottom bunk onto the floor.

Nate opened his eyes, confused. He took a deep breath. Why did he smell warm, cheesy tacos?

"What's that smell?" asked Yasu. He was sitting up and his hair stuck out in all different directions.

"What's in the bag, Carlos?" Vik asked.

"Tacos!" said Carlos. "Wake up or I'll eat 'em all myself." He turned on the lantern and pulled wrapped tacos out of a bag, tossing one taco to each boy, saying, "Think fast, buddy! Catch!"

Nate sat up, snagged a taco in mid-air, and looked down at Carlos in the dark. "Thanks," Nate said. "What time is it?"

"Taco time!" said Carlos. "It was my night off, so I went to town and brought back tacos for us all. I also got beans, sodas, chips, and guacamole. Get up and dig in, my friends."

"Yahoo!" cheered the boys. They jumped out of their beds and crowded around Carlos to get beans and sodas and to scoop up handfuls of chips to dip in the guacamole.

Holding his sloppy taco in one hand, Nate slipped off his bunk. His bird notebook slipped off at the same time, dropping into the darkness. He felt around for it with no luck, and decided to look for it later.

Now all of Birch Cabin was awake—except Simon, who could sleep though a train wreck. Vik, Jim, and Erik lounged on their beds, eating tacos and swigging sodas. Sean was doing a sleepy solo moonwalk, shuffling and kicking backward through the mess on the floor, waving one arm and crunching a taco all at the same time. Kareem was balancing a can of soda on his head as he walked heel-to-toe, as if he were on a tightrope.

"To Wolf Trail and its awesome campers," said Carlos, holding up his taco for a toast. He sat on Nate's trunk and plunked the greasy taco bag down next to him.

"What are we celebrating?" asked Yasu.

Carlos shrugged. "Nothing, everything," he said. "I'm sure every one of you guys has done something today that you're proud of, or found out something new about yourself. Celebrate that."

"Cheers!" the boys said.

Nate didn't have to ask himself what he was celebrating. He knew exactly: facing his fear of riding. He hadn't wanted to, but he'd made himself do it anyway. It was worth a silent taco toast to himself.

One by one, the boys toasted each other for goofy achievements, like Jim wearing the same shorts for six days in a row, and for semi-serious achievements, too, like Yasu always being the first one into the lake, or Kareem knowing every camp song, or Erik helping a guy who'd been homesick, or Vik turning out to be a natural around horses. They knocked together soda cans, spoons full of beans, and tacos. Then, sitting on their trunks or bunks or on the floor, the campers crunched and slurped like they had never been fed before.

When all had been eaten, down to the last beans and swipes of guacamole, and cold soda drained from the cans, Carlos strummed his guitar and sang to the tune of "Happy Birthday to You":

Happy tacos to you,
Soda, beans, and chips too.
Now you'll dream of guacamole,
And you'll sleep in it too.

The boys climbed back into their bunks and fell back asleep. Nate felt greasy, cheesy, full, and very happy.

"Word of the day, guys," sighed Zee. "Tah-coh-tah-coh-tah-coh-oh!"

Chapter Eight

Lying in his bunk the next morning, Nate peered through the screen out into the woods. *Crunch, crackle, plink.* A squirrel sat on a low branch in the morning sun, chewing the green hull of a black walnut, dropping chunks of the outer part on the ground as he worked his way to the tasty nut inside. *He's hungry 'cause he missed the tacos last night*, Nate thought, smiling. *He would have fit right in; he's a messy eater too.*

The cabin still smelled strongly—sort of reeked, actually—of taco sauce and cheese. Nate reached under the covers for his notebook. Not finding it, he hopped down from his bunk to the floor. Ouch! His legs ached from riding. *Where did I hide my notebook?* he asked himself, looking around the cabin, which was a disaster area. Nate turned to his trunk. Uh oh! Nate lifted the leaky leftover taco bag that was lying on his trunk. Sure enough, underneath the bag was his notebook. It was soaked with greasy orange taco sauce.

With the tips of two fingers, Nate lifted the notebook and moved it to the floor. He wiped it off with a towel, trying to blot up the sauce. That didn't work too well, so Nate slipped on his flip-flops and carried the notebook outside, hoping that he could find a hidden spot to let the notebook dry in the sun. Behind the cabin, near the edge of the woods, Nate found a wide tree stump. He did his best to peel apart the wet pages of the notebook without ripping them, and then he left the notebook open in the sun, walking back into Birch Cabin where his friends were just waking up.

★ ★ ★

After breakfast, the boys were ambling back to Birch Cabin. Erik was teaching them how to say *hello, good bye,* and *guacamole* in Norwegian, and Yasu was teaching them those same words in Japanese, when a brown streak shot past them, zooming down the path toward the dining hall. It was Cookie.

"You missed breakfast, Cookie!" teased Jim.

"Hey, Cookie!" called Zee. "Hello! Or in Japanese, '*Konnichiwa.*'"

Cookie stopped, turned, and wagged his tail.

"Look! Cookie speaks Japanese!" said Kareem.

"What's in his mouth?" asked Zack.

The dog gave them a guilty glance. As the boys started toward him, he backed away.

"Whatcha got, Cookie?" asked Nate. And then he saw. His notebook was sticking out of Cookie's mouth. "Aw, *man,* " groaned Nate. "He's got my notebook! Cookie! Hey, buddy, sit please." But as Nate approached Cookie, the dog took off like a rocket, bounding toward the dining hall. Nate chased him, calling, "Cookie, stop! Hey, *stop.*"

"C'mon," Erik hollered to the rest of the guys. "Let's help Nate."

Cookie led the boys down the twisting trail, darting between trees and leaping over fallen logs, all the way back to the dining hall. At the door of the dining hall, the dog skidded to a stop. He reached up with his front legs and pawed at the door, then with a flip of his ears, he nosed the door open and slipped inside. When the boys finally caught up, they found Cookie crouched under a table, licking the taco-sauce-flavored notebook.

"Stay, Cookie, stay," said Nate. He inched toward the dog.

Cookie lowered his head so that his drooly jaw rested on the notebook. He looked at Nate with big eyes.

"Hey, Cookie. Hey, buddy," cooed Zack. He knelt down and offered Cookie a piece of bacon left over from breakfast.

Cookie lifted his head and sniffed. Then cool as a cucumber, he crawled out from under the table and took the bacon from Zack's hand.

"Smart move," Nate said to Zack.

As Cookie ate, Zee dove under the table and

grabbed the notebook. "Got it!" he said.

"Thanks," said Nate, reaching for the notebook. "I'll—"

But just then, Kareem and Jim, who'd trailed the pack when the boys were chasing Cookie, burst through the door.

"What happened? What did we miss?" Jim gasped.

"Zack distracted Cookie with bacon," said Yasu. "And Zee rescued Nate's notebook. Or what's left of it."

Everybody looked at the notebook as Zee handed it to Nate.

"Bummer, Nate," said Kareem. "Cookie made dog chow out of your notebook."

Yasu leaned in and squinted at the notebook. "What is this anyway?" he asked. "You have drawings in here?"

"Sort of," said Nate. He felt his face getting hot. Which was worse? Having his notebook soaked in taco sauce, licked and chewed by a dog, or having his notebook recovered, which meant being discovered by his friends?

All of the boys crowded close, looking over Nate's shoulder at the sticky, chewed notebook. The cover was gone, so Nate couldn't hide the drawings on the first page. Nobody said anything. Nate thought he heard a woodpecker outside, banging its beak on a tree. Nate's head felt like he was banging *it* on a tree as he waited to be teased.

But Camp Wolf Trail had another one of its surprises in store for him. This time, it was a good one, not like finding out that he didn't like horses.

"Hey, I've seen that bird," said Jim, pointing to Nate's sketch.

"Me too," said Kareem. "I didn't know it was called a nuthatch."

"Look at the ducks," said Sean, pointing to another sketch.

"Those aren't ducks, you nuthatch," said Zee. "Look, it says right here: *geese*."

"Honkers, not quackers," said Vik.

"Let me see," said Yasu, leaning in.

Slam! The screen door swung shut as Skeeter

ran into the dining hall. "What's Cookie done now?" the cook asked as he mopped sweat from his face, which had gone cherry-red from running.

"Cookie ate Nate's notebook because it got soaked in grease and taco sauce from last night when Carlos brought us tacos," Erik explained in a rush. "And it's a lousy deal, because Nate had sketches of birds in the notebook."

"Here's another sketch," Vik said. He picked up a rumpled piece of paper from the floor and flattened it out on the table. "Pretty gross: dog slobber and taco sauce. But you can still kind of tell that it's an owl."

"You saw that owl that's been hooting sometimes?" asked Sean. "Cool."

"No, I—" Nate began.

But Skeeter interrupted him, saying solemnly, "Son, I am sorry that Cookie ruined your work."

"That's okay," Nate mumbled. "I mean, it's only a hobby."

"Whaddya mean, *only* a hobby?" said Kareem. "How come you never told any of us that you like birds?" Yasu asked.

Nate shrugged. "I guess I was afraid you'd laugh at me," he said. "The kids last year at school did, big time."

"We're not the kids at school," said Jim.

"They said it was dorky to like birds and know facts and stuff about them," Nate added.

"Hey, I know facts and stuff about animals," said Zack, "from my *Outdoor Guide* book. So if you're dorky, I am too, bro." He high-fived Nate.

"If knowing lots of anything makes you a dork, sign me up too," said Vik, "because I know millions of knock-knock jokes."

"How about me and how I know all the words to all the camp songs?" said Kareem.

"*Major* dorkdom."

"Do I get to qualify as a dork for my 'words-of-the-day'?" asked Zee. "Or for knowing the cowboy songs?"

"Okay, okay. I get it, " laughed Nate. It was great that all his friends now knew about how he liked birds, and even greater that they supported

Chapter Nine

For the next two days, Joe took the boys on short trail rides. Joe rode his horse, April, at the head of the line, and the rest of the horses followed along peacefully, only occasionally running into one another. Even so, Nate didn't like trail rides any better than he liked riding in circles inside the paddock. In fact, on the trail there were lots more things to worry about: getting whacked by low-hanging branches, getting your knee knocked on a tree, heaving forward when Herschel was going downhill, and falling backward when he was going uphill. Also, Herschel loved to stop and reach up and yank off leaves to nibble or bend down and rip up a big wad of grass to chew. The trailside evidently looked like an all-you-can-eat buffet

their horses forward, and slowly the horses fell into line again, following Joe on April as he led the way through the woods.

Although the sun had gone down completely, the sky wasn't black. Instead, it was a sickening gray—the color of smoke. The stars were hidden, but when he looked up, Nate could see what looked like a million fireflies lighting up the evening sky as sparks flew. The air reeked of smoke. It was so thick that it was hard to breathe, and it made Nate's eyes itchy and watery. Nate coughed. He tried to wipe his runny eyes on his sleeve without loosening his grip on the pommel, but he couldn't reach, and he didn't dare let go. Beneath him, Herschel was tense, but quiet. He moved forward cautiously. The other horses shook their heads and whinnied, sounding as if they were frightened.

Will's horse stumbled, and the horses in front and behind shied off right and left. "Talk to your horses, boys," said Joe. "Tell them it's going to be fine. When we get to the access road, we'll go straight down the mountain, no problem."

But it wasn't that simple.

As the riders got closer to the access road, Nate could see red lights flashing through the trees. Huge fire trucks clogged the road, and others were driving up, sirens screeching. Voices crackled on radios. Firefighters shouted to one another and swarmed up the road in packs. Across the narrow road, the fire burned its way down the mountain, consuming the trees in its path in an evil, unstoppable, wave of flames.

Still in the woods a few yards from the road, the riders stopped and gathered. Herschel planted his feet, but the other horses shifted their weight restlessly, and jerked their heads up and down, terrified by the noise and chaos on the access road.

"Follow me," ordered Joe. He had to shout to be heard. Joe squeezed April and spoke to her gently, but she moved sideways and refused to go forward toward the road.

Nate saw Simon's horse toss his head. His neck was covered with sweat, and he acted like he was about to explode. The horse's anxiety was contagious. It spread from horse to horse like a sort of fire itself. All the horses except Herschel danced and acted fretful. They balked when the boys tried to make them walk forward. Not one horse would move toward the road.

Suddenly, Yasu swung off his horse and stood on his own two feet.

Joe turned around in the saddle. "Yasu, what are you doing?" he shouted.

"She's too scared," Yasu said of his horse. "I'm going to lead her."

"Get back on that horse," said Joe. "Now!"

Yasu tried, but his high-strung horse wouldn't let him remount. With Yasu on the ground, the rest of the horses seemed more unnerved than ever. Then a burning tree crashed, sending embers sparking up, and Simon's horse reared and bucked, throwing Simon to the ground.

"Simon's down!" shouted Vik. He had to yell for Joe to hear him above the sirens and the thunder of the helicopter that was now circling above the trees.

Joe jumped off April and ran to help Simon. Simon stood up and dusted himself off. He grimaced, holding his back, and tried to grab his horse's reins. But his horse ran loose, charging back and forth across the trail between the other horses and upsetting them.

Joe handed April's reins to Simon. "Stay with April!" he said. Then, talking in a soothing voice and walking slowly forward, Joe managed to get hold of Simon's horse's reins and calm him. But now there were three riders off their horses, and precious time had been lost. Nate could feel Herschel trembling beneath him, though he was the only horse standing still. All the others shuffled, trying to turn away from the road.

Suddenly, Joe turned to Nate. "We've got to get out of here," he said. "I need you to make Herschel walk out of these woods and onto the access road. The other horses will follow Herschel. Can you do it, son?"

Chapter Ten

No! Nate wanted to shout. *Not me! I can't! I'm the shakiest rider here.* He had never been so overcome with fear in his life. His heart pounded, his hands shook, and his teeth chattered.

All the boys looked at Nate, their faces pale and frightened. Even Vik looked worried, though he tried to grin encouragingly at Nate. Just then, Nate remembered what Vik had said to him before: *Doing what you're scared of? That's brave.*

Nate took a shuddery breath. He did not want to let his friends down. Slowly, but definitely, he nodded at Joe. "I'll do it," he said.

Joe nodded back. "It's up to you, Nate."

Nate leaned forward and patted Herschel's

neck. *Joe's wrong. It's not up to me,* he said to his horse without speaking. *It's up to you, Herschel. Just think of me as one of those cowbirds. They trust you, and I do too. Let's go.*

Nate squeezed with his legs and asked Herschel to walk toward the road. Herschel pointed his ears forward, then took a step forward, and then another.

"Good boy," said Nate. He was scared, but if Herschel could put one foot in front of the other and walk toward the noise and commotion, the smoke and the blood-red lights, and the dust whorls whipped up by the helicopter, then Nate could face it too. Nate looked back to check on the others. He could see the tense faces of the boys as they whispered calming, encouraging words to their horses. Nate was glad to see that the other horses *were* following Herschel, even if only reluctantly, and with hesitant steps.

The lights from the fire trucks illuminated the road so Nate could see it through the trees. He pushed back the tree branches that scraped and clawed at his face, snapping them the best he could to make the path a little more clear for everyone behind him. He was so focused on clearing the way to the road for the others that he didn't feel the scrapes or the cuts from the sharp branches that scratched his arms. Meanwhile, Herschel plodded steadily forward, leading the line of skittish horses.

Step-by-step, inch-by-inch, Nate and Herschel led the line of horses out of the woods. When they emerged onto the road, Nate turned right sharply and kept Herschel as close as he could to the edge, as far away from the fire trucks and commotion as possible.

Then Herschel walked cautiously down the access road. With every step they took away from the fire and the racket and the smoke, Nate's heart beat more slowly. Above them, gradually the night sky cleared, giving them just enough moonlight to find their way.

No one spoke. The sirens grew fainter behind them and soon, the only sounds were the gentle *clinks* of the horses' bridles and the soft thud of their hooves on the dusty road. Steady and steadfast, Herschel led the tired group back to Camp Wolf Trail, then along the path to the farm. By now the horses had picked up their pace and seemed to know they were headed home. Behind the riders, Joe and Yasu were on foot, leading their horses. Last of all was Simon, leading his horse and limping a bit, bringing up the rear.

Silently, the riders entered the paddock. One by one, they slid off their exhausted horses onto the grassy ground. They set to work taking off the saddles, rubbing their horses down, giving them water, and settling them for the night.

When they were finished, Joe said, "Good job, men. I'm proud of you."

"Thanks, Joe," the boys said.

Vik spoke up. "Thank you too, Nate," he said. "You and Herschel got us home safely."

All the boys murmured in agreement. "Yeah, thanks, Nate," they said.

Nate felt so pleased and proud that he was grinning from ear to ear. "Thank Herschel," he said. "He did it. All I did was sit on his back."

★ ★ ★

First thing the next morning, before breakfast, Nate and Vik walked over to the farm.

Simon and Joe were in the paddock, checking all the horses to be sure they were okay after their adventure the night before.

"Let me guess, you want to see Herschel?" Simon asked when he saw Nate and Vik.

The boys nodded.

"Herschel is fine," said Simon as they walked toward him. "Healthy as a horse, you know the old saying." Simon looked at Nate and said earnestly, "You and Herschel made a pretty good team on that ride, Nate. Impressive."

"Thanks," said Nate. He patted Herschel's neck.

Joe spoke up. "I've got some good news," he said. "First of all, the fire is out. Secondly, I got some emails from people wanting to adopt horses. Looks like we might find homes for Christmas

Wish, the grays, and the chestnuts, at least."

"Cool," said Vik.

"What about Herschel?" asked Nate, resting his hand on Herschel's shoulder.

Joe seemed to be trying not to laugh. "Yeah, got some crazy coot who wants Herschel, believe it or not," he said.

"Seriously?" asked Nate happily. "Is he a nice guy?"

Now Joe burst out laughing. "Ask him yourself," he said. He pointed at Simon.

"You?" asked Nate and Vik together.

"Yeah," said Simon. "I've decided to use the money I earn as a counselor this summer to adopt Herschel. He'll be great at my mom's school. She needs smart, steady, gentle horses because some of the kids she teaches are disabled. Good old Herschel proved beyond a doubt last night that he's unflappable, so he'll be a good starter horse for kids who are beginners, or kids who are iffy about riding."

"Or scared stiff, like me," said Nate.

Pffffft, snorted Herschel. It sounded exactly as if he was saying, *Cut it out, Nate. You're not scared anymore.*

Nate laughed, but he had to agree.

★ ★ ★

Vik and Nate walked back to camp together.

"The Isabels are going to be happy when we tell them that Simon is taking Herschel," said Vik.

"Yeah," said Nate. "And—"

Just then a shadow sped across the sunlight on the path. Out of the trees swooped the largest owl Nate had ever seen. Its gray and brown feathers whooshed over their heads as the owl passed them on quiet wings. Then, as quickly as it had appeared, the owl disappeared into the woods.

Vik gasped, and Nate said, "Whoa! Did you see that? *That* is what they call a flying tiger."

"Want to follow it and try to find it in the woods?" asked Vik.

"Nah," said Nate. "Now that I've seen the owl itself, I don't need to see where it lives." He grinned. "It's okay with me if the owl wants to keep that a secret. I don't have any secrets left myself, anymore."

"Right!" said Vik. "Everybody knows about how you're crazy for the birds, and after last night, you being scared of horses isn't true anymore. No more secrets."

"Unless you have one," Nate said. He was tossing the still unopened owl pellet from hand to hand. "Which I think you do."

Vik slid him a sideways, smiling glance. "Good thing you've got the rest of our time here at camp to find out," he said.

REAL BOYS CAMP STORIES

Ray Danner

Ray Danner is a biologist who studies how animals interact with each other and their environment, how they evolve over time, and how they can be conserved. He is specifically interested in migratory birds and endangered birds that live on islands. For his research, he spends a large amount of time outdoors watching wildlife and dreaming about that when he is sitting inside at his computer.

It was after dark and Dad was leading us on a night hike. Our less brave friends and family had stayed to watch the campfire, but we wanted adventure. We wanted to explore nature. We had left our camp in the forest and now stood on a beach along the river. We turned off our flashlights and looked around. A big moon hung in the sky and we could see just like it was daytime. The rocks all around us looked white in the moonlight, and I thought, *This is what the surface of the moon must look like.* I could see my mom's smile and my sister's eyes widen as a shooting star flew overhead. The water was clear even at night, and was beautiful, sliding like silk between the smooth rocks.

Night hikes were full of discoveries. If we stomped our feet on the rocks, they sparked. Our dad said these were the flint rocks that our ancestors used to start fires. Suddenly, a bat flew low over our heads, and I ducked. Some people would be scared, but we knew the bats were only chasing moths for their dinner, so we weren't afraid. Along the edge of the river, crayfish rocked back and forth gently in the small waves. When we tried to catch them, they raced into deeper water. At night crayfish seemed to be everywhere in the water, but we never saw them during the day. *Where do they go?* we wondered.

When it was time to return to camp, Dad asked me to lead the way. I was a little scared, because I wasn't sure I would remember the route. But I was proud my dad trusted me to lead, so I agreed. After a few wrong turns, we made it safely back to camp and the cozy beds in our tents.

Exploration and adventures like these were highlights of my childhood and are highlights of my life as a scientist today. Since I was very young, my parents took my little sister and me camping for a month every summer. We would load the car with a tent, sleeping bags, fishing and cooking gear, and a canoe. Then we'd drive to the Ozark Mountains and camp in the endless forests along rivers. Playing in the wild made me curious about how the natural world works and taught me how to be independent—both important qualities for a scientist.

Night hikes were just one of our many adventures. One day, after breakfast, I swam with a school of fish, trying hard to keep up with their quick movements. At lunch, I saw a rare bird dive powerfully into the water and spear one of those fast fish, making my sandwich seem boring. That afternoon, we caught insects and noticed their beautiful colors before letting them go. After dinner, as I neared the edge of our campsite, eyes of an unknown animal shined back at me in the dark. I wondered if this animal was friendly or not.

When I was older, I went to summer camp where there were new challenges. One summer we rode horses. The horses were impressive with their sleek, shiny hair and strong muscles. Their strength scared me too. I had never been on a horse and was worried that instead of walking, it would gallop and buck me off its back. One day we were on a long trail ride. Our horses were in a long single-file line, walking slowly. I was tired and about to fall asleep. All of a sudden, my horse left the line, trotted down a steep hill to a stream, and began to drink! After it was done, I pulled the reins to the left, and to my surprise, comfortably rode the horse back to the group.

Watching and interacting with animals while camping and at summer camp made me want to understand how they work. I wanted to know how bats catch insects in the dark and where crayfish go during the day. I wanted to know how birds could catch fast fish and why some insects are so colorful and others are not. Today, I still ask questions like these and use science to answer them.

As a scientist, I spend as much time as possible outdoors watching animals. By watching animals closely, we can learn how they work. I study birds. I study little birds and big birds, dull birds and bright birds. I study birds in the summer and birds in the winter. I study birds near my home and birds in far away places. To study birds, I have camped in forests in Alaska and Canada, on secluded beaches in Hawaii, and in the mountains of Central and South America. In each of these places, I've explored and had adventures, and feel just as excited and curious as when I was young.

I encourage everyone to get out and experience life in the wild. This does not require camping on secluded riverbanks in the Ozarks Mountains or jungles in South America. It does not even require camping! In your backyard or in the park down the street, plants and animals are doing a lot of exciting things! They are finding food, growing, and having kids of their own. They help one another and sometimes fight. Weather is constantly changing, stars shoot across the sky. You can take part in the exploration and adventure of learning about these things by simply spending time outside your door. And who knows, maybe you'll want to be a scientist too.

On behalf of the birds he loves so much, Ray has donated the proceeds from this essay to the Migratory Bird Center based at the Smithsonian's National Zoo in Washington, DC. Find out who the bird of the month is (and more) at http://nationalzoo.si.edu/scbi/migratorybirds.

Stick the **BIRD IDENTIFICATION CARD** from the back of your book in your back pocket and start looking for birds!

Keep a Lookout for Birds:

·in the sky ·in the trees ·on the pond ·in a park

·on wires ·under bridges ·on the ground ·on rooftops ·at the beach

Fine, Feathered Friends

Use a felt-tip pen to put a check next to the birds you see on your ID CARD.

Home Tweet Home

Make nesting birds welcome by providing short pieces of string, yarn, or rags hanging from branches. They also like dog hair, lint, and dried grass.

Make a bird bath by filling an upside-down garbage can lid or shallow pail with pebbles and water.

Make a bird house by hanging a basket or wooden box from a tree or hook.

Cheep Trills

Listen for quacks, honks, whistles, chirps, and clicks.

Try to imitate the bird sounds that you hear.

Curl your tongue, fill it with spit, and whistle. Hooting owl, right?

Beaks 'n Bills

The shape of a bird's bill tells you what it eats and how it eats it. Try to find birds with beaks and bills that are hooked, cone-shaped, flat and wide, expandable, or tubular.

Birds of a Feather

Not all groups of birds are called flocks. Geese gather in gaggles; crows crowd in murders; swans swim in wedges; larks rise in exaltations; jays bond in bands; and owls—well, why don't you make up a name for a group of owls yourself?